A BOOK OF SHADOWS COLLECTION

# THE DAMNATION CHRONICLES

*Companion Stories*

# MICHAEL PENNING

THE DAMNATION CHRONICLES

First edition. October, 2022
ISBN: 978-1-7781523-4-4 (paperback)

www.michaelpenning.com

*Author's Note*

This companion story to the *Book of Shadows* novels takes place before the events of *All Hallows Eve*, but can be enjoyed at any time.

## A Firebrand of Hell

Rebecca Hale knelt in her cell and cursed the people of Salem. They reviled her and branded her an enemy of God. She was the one who tormented the poor village girls. She was the witch who blighted the harvest. Rebecca Hale rode the midnight winds and brought sickness and death to the innocent. The Puritans of Salem had condemned her and made her suffer, and now she damned them all to Hell.

"If it be blood they crave, let them drink blood 'till mine be repaid," she rasped through lips that were cracked and raw.

Rebecca had once been pretty, but her teeth were now sickly yellow. The freckles of her face and arms were now obscured by grime smeared across her pale skin. Her thick red hair was a tangled mess of impossible knots and her mouth was a dry crack stretched between two sunken cheeks. Dull green eyes stared from the depths of hollow sockets like tarnished emeralds tossed in a well. The limp remains of a simple black gown hung from her emaciated frame, the linen now little more than soiled rags.

Imprisoned in a chamber no wider than an upright coffin, Rebecca had crouched low enough to kneel on the filthy floor. It was her only respite from endless hours standing upright. There wasn't room for a chair or bed. Lying across the floor to sleep was impossible. Rebecca's only luxury was a tin pail for her waste. Above where she knelt, slivers of feeble candlelight flickered through rusty iron bars set into the oaken door. Some villagers had questioned wasting good candles on such wicked prisoners, but Edgar Fisk had been adamant.

Salem's jailor was a brutish blacksmith who blamed the witches for his wife's death. He was the first to volunteer to keep them behind bars—and to serve as a hangman if needed. Fisk knew what horrors the witches were capable of; he wouldn't leave them alone in the dark to work their evil. Each evening, while the dying light of dusk still glowed through the jail's only window, the jailor descended into the dungeon to set a candle on a ledge in the narrow stone corridor.

The air down there was so cold and damp that water ran down the walls in thin but constant trickles, leaving behind sticky streams of rusty orange mildew. The candle's fragile flame sent a tendril of oily black smoke up into the darkness that shrouded the ancient beams of the ceiling. In the gathering gloom, the weak light gave off no warmth and no consolation. The stench of unwashed bodies, filth, and mold that permeated the cavernous dungeon overpowered the sour scent of the tallow wax.

Some nights, Fisk's candle burned itself out more quickly than others. Fisk never dared to venture down into the black depths of the dungeon to replace it. He had thought about it once. He'd even lit a new candle and stood peering down the steep staircase into the murky darkness below. The candlelight illuminated the first few rickety steps. The rest vanished into a gaping pool of blackness. Somewhere down there, Fisk could hear the witches breathing, moaning, whispering. What were they doing down there? Conjuring? Communing with the devil?

Fisk had glanced down to find the candle shaking in his hand. His nerve failed and his feet felt rooted to the floor. He couldn't will himself to take a single step down that staircase. With a shudder, he slammed the heavy door and slid the bolt home, checking it twice. Despite his misgiving about leaving the witches alone in the dark, some nights it was safer to leave them be and pray he was worthy of God's protection.

Tonight would be one of those nights.

Rebecca huddled beneath the sputtering rays of Fisk's dying candle and whimpered to herself as she waited for the dreaded darkness. Of all the terrors she had suffered in the months since her arrest, it was the darkness she feared most.

That's when *he* came to her. The Dark Man.

Rebecca's vacant gaze roamed over a jumble of scratches streaked across the stone walls on all sides of her. She no longer knew how long they had imprisoned her, and she no longer cared. She knew only that three nights had passed since she had gouged those walls with her nails—the night another wretched victim of the town's hysteria had died in a neighboring cell.

Ann Foster's body had remained rotting in the squalor for almost a day before anyone noticed that her soul had moved on. Through the narrow bars of her door, Rebecca watched in horror as the first rat materialized from the shadows. It came scurrying down the dingy corridor, a large, filthy creature with loathsome eyes and diseased flesh. More vermin followed, drawn from the nearby harbor by the enticing scent of the newly dead. Rebecca heard their chatter as they fed on Ann's remains in the night's silence.

Until that moment, Rebecca had handled her long ordeal with relative dignity and even a degree of measured contempt for her persecutors. But the revolting sound of the rats glutting themselves on the dead woman was enough to snap the final shreds of Rebecca's sanity. Driven mad by weeks of isolation, claustrophobia, and terror, she had thrown herself at the walls of her tiny cell, spinning around in desperate circles, rebounding from one wall to another and clawing at the stone as if it were skin she could sink her nails into and tear away.

"*Ann Foster is dead!*" she wailed. "Please! She is being devoured! Somebody please have mercy on her! Please! *Oh God, please deliver me!*"

Rebecca had screamed and flayed at the walls for hours, oblivious to the searing pain shooting up her manacled wrists as her fingernails tore loose and tumbled to the ground at her feet. Other inmates raised their voices and joined her, but screams were common in the witch jail and Edgar Fisk no longer paid them any attention. Exhausted, Rebecca had crumpled to the floor and sold herself to despair. She wept as her unraveling mind retraced the days to the moment her terrible ordeal had begun... her wedding day.

It was the first proper day of spring. After a long and bitter winter, the gentle breezes carried the fresh scent of blooming lilacs from the nearby pasture. Life was being renewed. On that warm May morning, Rebecca reveled in its fragrance, gratified by the certainty that her life was about to change. Little did she know the horrible direction it was about to take.

The sounds of her children going about their chores bounced through Rebecca's humble cottage. John and the other boys were outside stacking firewood. The chore made John's brothers feel like they were men. It reminded them of the father that had gone missing months ago and was now presumed dead. Mary and Sarah were busy kneading the dough for the day's bread while Susannah minded the littlest one, who seemed determined to climb on every available surface.

Alone in the privacy of the cottage's only walled room, Rebecca turned to where her Sunday dress hung from a wooden peg and let her eyes move over it. She had spent a considerable amount for the expensive black dyes she'd used to color the plain brown linen. As a widow, it was only proper that she should wear black when she remarried. Rebecca considered herself a proper woman despite what some in the village said about her. They thought her a hellion who led godly young men to corruption and vice, drinking and playing at shovelboard at unseemly hours at the tavern she owned on the Ipswich Road. Her marriage to her first husband, Philip, worsened her infamy. Theirs had been a tumultuous one and violence was not uncommon. Once, she and Philip had both been brought to court for fighting.

"She hath appeared at one time bloody and other times black and blue," a neighbor testified. "She hath also given her husband several blows."

Rebecca and Philip had confessed to fighting to avoid a whipping. They were made to stand back-to-back and gagged in the public market for half a day as punishment. When Philip went missing months later, Rebecca heard the disturbing rumors being whispered among her neighbors: she was a witch who had set a hex upon her husband.

Rebecca pushed these unwanted memories aside as she took the dress from the peg, stepped into her skirt, and secured it around her waist. The long, black folds fell to her ankles. She laced her bodice and savored the way the fabric hugged her body. She had worn this same dress every Sunday for years, but somehow today it felt different. It was warm and supple in ways it had never been before.

Rebecca found herself blushing as she admired the way the delicate black linen framed her from chest to waist. Surprised by her own unexpected vanity, her freckled cheeks bloomed with a warm pink flush. She knew her marriage to Thomas Carrier was merely one of convenience for them both. Yet she still wanted to impress him. Was it gratitude for the pity he had taken on her? He had been friends with Rebecca's first husband. When Phillip had disappeared, Thomas felt compelled to care for his friend's family as his own, regardless of Rebecca's unsavory reputation. A respected merchant who had been working so hard to attain his position that he had never taken the time to marry, he now needed a wife to tend to his house. God-willing, Rebecca would also bear him a son. For her part, Rebecca needed a man to teach her boys to hunt, to help tend the cattle and crops, and to maintain the upkeep of their house.

And while her tavern had kept her financially secure since Philip's disappearance, Rebecca hated the scorn she met for keeping it. She hated the long nights away from her children and the shame she suffered for the pleasure of her male patrons. But what other choice did she have? How else was she expected to provide for her seven children? When Thomas proposed marriage, it was as if an enormous weight had lifted. He was a good man who worked hard and owned a successful business.

Rebecca was excited to be married to a man who was so well-respected. It was the chance for a *decent* life, one in which she could put the memories of her sordid past behind her. With Thomas as her husband, she could sell the tavern and put its old ghosts to rest.

What Rebecca still could not admit to herself was that she now felt a genuine affection for Thomas. Perhaps even love. He made her feel wanted again, something she hadn't felt in years.

A smile came to Rebecca's lips as she reached for her bonnet. A sound froze her on her way to the door.

A horse was approaching.

Rebecca paused and listened. Thomas? So soon? No, the man was foolish for traditions. He wouldn't want to see his bride before the wedding. Magistrate Stoughton? It couldn't be. The ceremony was still hours away; he would be much too early.

This rider was not expected.

Rebecca felt an awful sense of foreboding as the slow pounding of hooves grew louder. Her thoughts strayed to the turmoil sweeping the townspeople. Salem was ablaze with dreadful talk of witchcraft. Some of the village girls had fallen into fits—shrieking in agony, writhing on the floor, contorting themselves into grotesque poses. Reverend Parris proclaimed them tormented by witchcraft, and soon the accusations had begun. Fear imbued every whisper. Suspicions were rampant. Neighbors cast sidelong glances at each other. Some said the Devil himself had come to Salem.

Rebecca knew the villagers would soon see the afflicted girls for the liars they were. If the Devil walked among the people of Salem, it wasn't in the company of that gaggle of unruly firebrands. It was one thing to have convinced the God-fearing reverend they were bewitched; Parris saw evil spirits in every stray wind that blew through town. But now Justice Hathorne himself was indulging their outrageous fits and delusions as well. Rebecca and Hathorne had crossed paths often enough at her tavern. She knew him well—or at least she thought she did. If they could no longer count on Hathorne, someone else would soon have the sense to end the girls' bothersome nonsense.

And yet, more arrests were being made. Examinations were being held...

Rebecca had resolved to keep her opinions to herself. Few people knew the mind of a town like a tavern-keeper, and Rebecca sensed the mind of Salem was clouded by paranoia. A storm was brewing, and while she knew in her heart it would blow over, she also felt it wiser to remain on higher ground until it did. Too much had already happened. It was becoming apparent that to speak out against the afflicted girls was to provoke their fury.

Now, with the sound of hoofbeats drawing ever nearer, an icy chill stole up Rebecca's spine and into her throat. Her fingers trembled and her breath shook in her lungs as she struggled to calm herself, telling herself the rider could be anyone. Perhaps a neighbor arriving to wish her well before her wedding? Some in this town still called her friend.

But the reassuring thought rang hollow, even to herself.

Something was wrong. That rider shouldn't be here.

Rebecca's heart raced and her pulse throbbed in her neck as a sickening feeling settled in the pit of her stomach. She thought of the village girls, their horrible accusations...

The trembling in Rebecca's fingers had now spread throughout her body. The familiar spot on the floorboards creaked as she crossed over them to the window. She dreaded what she would find there and prayed she would be wrong. Her hand shook as she held her breath and drew back the curtains.

Riding up the lane was Sheriff Corwin.

Rebecca saw the roll of parchment clutched in the sheriff's hand. It was a warrant. She gasped. In one terrible instant, her worst fears had come true.

They had accused her.

Corwin drew nearer, a dreadful black specter cutting through the exploding colors of the apple blossoms. Each beat of his horse's hooves rang out like the Lord's own hammer, pronouncing Rebecca's doom. At the sight of him, her heart sank to a bottomless depth from which it never returned. Her knees buckled and the sick feeling in her stomach released itself into an awful wave of panic. Hot tears sprang to her eyes as she shrank away from the window, her mind racing for answers. The sounds from the kitchen had fallen silent. Rebecca's children had heard the rider approaching as well.

*Her children...*

The room suddenly felt too small, her dress too constricting. She felt like a prisoner when the diamond shadows cast by the windowpane fell on her. The air was sucked from her lungs. Her mind plunged toward a dark oblivion as the walls spun around her. There was a sharp knock at the front door, but Rebecca thought it was from far away. She staggered across the room, reached for the dresser, and missed. The floorboards rushed up to meet her and the world went black as her mind embraced the welcome solace of unconsciousness.

The months that followed were a series of blurred impressions as one bizarre and impossible event gave way to the next, like the surreal twists of a dream dissolving into a nightmare. Days after her arrest, Rebecca found herself at the meetinghouse being examined by Justice Hathorne.

"They say you have bewitched thy husband to death." The judge's voice scraped through the dry gravel of his throat. "His body hath been found eaten by wolves by the Northern Woods —bloodthirsty familiars of thine own conjuring. What say you?"

Rebecca fixed with him a defiant glare. "I know nothing of it. I am no witch."

Each time she denied the judge's accusations of witchcraft, the afflicted girls would fall to their knees, screaming and writhing in agony. Ann Putnam twisted her limbs into impossible angles and wailed that Rebecca's spirit was tearing her apart. Mercy Lewis attempted to twist her own head around to the point of snapping. Mary Warren pointed at Rebecca and cried that she could see the devil at her ear, whispering curses from his black book.

Too shocked to move, Rebecca watched in disbelief as people

leaped to the aid of the shrieking girls, soothing them, comforting them, embracing them. For the first time, she witnessed their awful power, and terror gripped her heart. The girls wailed and thrashed on the meetinghouse floor and Rebecca came to the horrifying realization that her innocence was worthless. What could she say to defend herself against such a wicked performance? Even the sanest among them believed in the testimonies of fiends.

The nightmare twisted and Rebecca found herself flung into a squalid cell and chained to the wall in irons. At dawn one dismal morning, they snatched her and led down the foul corridor to a small stone chamber. They stripped naked and made to stand on a rickety chair to be searched for witchmarks. Exposed and ashamed, she stood trembling in the cold as the calloused hands of Edgar Fisk probed every inch of her naked flesh. A greasy leer slid across his face as he paid particular attention to her most delicate areas.

In the months since Philip's disappearance, Rebecca had endured countless indignities at the hands of the men who frequented her tavern. But now, unable to stand the sheer humiliation of the jailor's hands slithering across her skin, her mind fled. The stone walls of the dismal room dissolved around her. She was no longer a captive in the depths of the witch dungeon. She was in the vast meadow she had played in as a girl. Bright honey-yellow sunshine poured itself across rolling acres of tall grass that brushed across her ankles. The aroma of milkweed filled the air—syrupy and spicy and dripping with memories of her youth. Lush fields of violets and prairie asters spread before her, a riot of blues and whites. The soft and vivid spires of lupines swayed in the breeze and cascaded down a gentle hillside before giving way to the tall thickets of silky pussy-willows and orange lilies that stretched along the banks of the clear, cool brook. A flight of swallows soared and swirled above her. Rebecca closed her eyes and sank to her knees, glorying in their music.

Countless days sped by. Rebecca's mind continued to flee

with every new degradation. She watched herself from a distance, from somewhere in the meadow, as if it was all happening to someone else, someone she didn't know. In her rare lucid moments, Rebecca often wondered what had become of her children. She had demanded they not visit her. There were dangerous rumors swirling through the village. Some believed her children were the devil's progeny, conceived during her witch Sabbaths in the Northern Woods. No matter the heartache it brought her, Rebecca refused to risk their safety by seeing them. The power of Salem's afflicted girls was now fearfully absolute—and children were not beyond the aim of their accusations.

Summer came and went by the time they hauled Rebecca back before Judge Hathorne. On trial for her life, she watched with that now familiar sense of detachment as they led her accusers into the meetinghouse. They fell into hysterics at the sight of her. Rebecca's spirit was biting them, choking them, burning them, drowning them. Hathorne seemed to observe their suffering with a sense of satisfaction. There was no need to prove Rebecca's guilt; it was obvious for all to see. Hathorne seemed fixed on a hanging and the hysterical girls were sure to give him one. With absolute horror, Rebecca saw her last hope for salvation slip away as she came to understand why the judge was so intent on seeing her hang. It was because of the dark secret they both shared.

While the afflicted girls shrieked and writhed, Hathorne hammered Rebecca with a barrage of dreadful accusations. "Does it trouble you to see these innocents thus tormented?"

"No," Rebecca murmured.

"How is it that thy appearance doth hurt these?"

"I know not. I am innocent." Rebecca's mumbled answers became more and more distracted as her mind left her accusers behind and soared from the meetinghouse to the warm relief of her meadow.

It was now the hour of midnight. The sour smell of Ann Foster's death still lingered on the stale air of the fetid jail as

Rebecca knelt in her filthy cell and muttered curses to herself. The yellow stench of sickness had joined the stale reek. It was a scent Rebecca knew too well. One of the poor souls down the corridor wouldn't live long enough to face her accusers at her trial. Whoever it was would be dead within days, and the vile rats would return.

Rebecca was grateful they would spare her such a miserable fate.

In the morning, she would hang instead.

A sputtering hiss came from the corridor beyond her cell door as Fisk's candle went out. Engulfed in the darkness, Rebecca gasped with fright and cringed at her sudden blindness. With her senses heightened, the wretched moans of nearby cells rang in her ears. Her heart thundered like the pounding hooves of Sheriff Corwin's horse on the fateful day of her arrest. She slumped against a wall and closed her eyes, praying for a sleep she knew wouldn't come. Instead, her thoughts drifted as they always did to her children.

At dawn, they would be orphans. What would become of Mary, her eldest child? Would she take on the duties of caring for her younger siblings? Would they force her to walk the same shameful path that Rebecca had to support them? And what of ten-year-old John? Had he already taken to the dreadful game some of the other boys his age played? When they dared each other to climb the gallows tree to see if they could set a witch's corpse to spinning? Did her children still hold fast to her innocence? Or had they turned on her to spare themselves, just as Thomas had done? Part of Rebecca wished they had. She could face the gallows with serenity and grace if she knew they were safe.

*Shall I show you thy children?*

A voice uncoiled from the darkness. It was deep and resonant and haunting.

The hairs rose on Rebecca's neck and the blood turned to ice in her veins. She wasn't alone.

The Dark Man was there with her.

A chill crawled over Rebeca's skin. Terror raced through her heart as she shrank into a corner and wrapped her arms around her knees. She squeezed her eyes shut and willed him to be gone, but she could still feel him there, an unholy presence lurking close but unseen in the shadows.

"No, no, no, no, no…." she moaned. "I want none of you."

*On the morrow, thou shall become the grim fruit of the gallows tree. Wouldst thou know thy children's fate before you hang?*

A fierce and righteous rebuke leapt to Rebecca's lips, but she never let it loose. Instead, she faltered. After months of torment and heartbreak, she now found herself so very weary—too weary to withstand the Dark Man's temptations any longer. On the eve of her execution, she was alone and terribly afraid. Her strength and resolve failed her, and an irresistible yearning to see her children one last time overcame her. Throughout her imprisonment, her one source of courage had been her hope for their safety. It had sustained her through darkness and torment and humiliation. She had to know what would become of them after her death.

"Yes. Please, show me."

*Close thine eyes.*

Rebecca did as he asked.

What the Dark Man showed her shattered her heart and broke her spirit.

She was being chased through the dense fog of a thick woods. Sharp rocks tore into her bare feet as she raced through the underbrush. Skeletal tree limbs tore at her exposed skin. A gnarled root snared her ankle and gave it a nasty twist. A bolt of pain shot up her leg as she tripped, stumbled, and pitched to the forest floor. Sprawled in the blanket of dead leaves, she heard the heavy footfalls of men chasing her, moving fast. Their shouts echoed off the trees and came from all around her. She sprang to her feet and ran on, too terrified to feel the stabbing jolts darting from her swelling ankle. With her heart pounding in her chest, she raced through the woods until the trees ended and she burst into a small hollow where she stopped dead.

The lifeless bodies of seven little children hung from the trees, their heads covered with burlap sacks.

Rebecca's face contorted with anguish as her eyes flew open to release herself from the Dark Man's vision. She heard a hysterical voice shrieking and realized it was her own. Her sorrowful wails pierced the silence and echoed through the dungeon.

*Wouldst thou save them?*

The Dark Man's words struck Rebecca like cold water to her face and brought her grief-stricken sobs to an instant halt. A silence fell in the darkness as she remained quiet.

*Wouldst thou have me deliver thy children from harm?*

Rebecca quaked with fright. What was she thinking? This was unspeakably wicked. A prayer flew to her lips, but in her heart, she knew God had abandoned her long ago. All she had left were the Dark Man's promises and her own ferocious instinct to protect her children at all costs. She was powerless against it. From the moment the midwife had put Mary in her arms—pink and naked and shivering—Rebecca had braved untold hardships for the sake of her children. She had sheltered them from the storm of her first husband. When she had no other choice, she had sold her own body to keep them fed. She would sacrifice anything to keep them safe. Anything.

Even her soul.

"What wilt thou from me?" she whispered.

*One hundred years of servitude for one night of vengeance in my name.*

There was a rustling in the darkness. An ancient book slid across the floor into view. It was bound all in black and lay open at Rebecca's feet.

*Pledge thy body and soul to me and to none other.*

Rebecca wavered a moment, but she knew she had already made her choice. She couldn't let the Dark Man's terrible vision come to pass. The fate of her children hung on what she did in this very moment.

Her fingers trembled in the air as she reached for the black book.

An unseen hand took hers in the darkness.

Rebecca recoiled and almost snatched her hand away. But the Dark Man's hand was warm around hers and she hadn't known warmth in so very long. A pen was pressed into her palm. It was hard and heavy, as if forged of iron. The warm hand guided the pen's sharp nib down toward the tender flesh of Rebecca's wrist and she understood what it meant for her to do. Her fingers shook as she pierced the skin and drew blood, wincing as a bright prick of pain flashed up her arm. She lowered the crimson nib to the open page and scratched her bloody mark in the Dark Man's book.

The warm hand released Rebecca's. She felt the tattered remains of her soiled dress slipping off each of her thin and wasted shoulders. She clutched her hands to her chest, but the warm hand gently brushed them aside. The dress fell away and smooth fingers caressed her breast. They were hot to the touch. A searing jolt shot through Rebecca as if she had been branded. She flinched, but there was also a tender pleasure in the touch. A breathless sigh escaped her lips.

Without warning, the Dark Man was gone. Rebecca was alone.

Goosebumps rose on her exposed skin and she shivered as she pulled her dress back up around her shoulders to conceal the Dark Man's mark. She rested her head against the cold stone. Her great weariness washed over her and dragged her deep under its waves. Her eyes slid closed and for the first time in many months, Rebecca's sleep was one of dreams instead of nightmares. Her meadow was lush and flourishing in the afternoon sun. Her children were running and playing in the wildflowers. Their laughter was music as Rebecca watched them from a distance, savoring the moment and wanting nothing more than to live in it forever.

But there was now a debt to be paid, a century of torment before she would have her revenge on the people of Salem—before she would claim their children as her own.

They would hang her for witchcraft at dawn. And so a witch she had become.

*Author's Note*

This companion story to the *Book of Shadows* novels takes place between the events of *All Hallows Eve* and *The Suicide Lake,* but can be enjoyed at any time.

## The Witch of Gallows Hill

The dead were all around her. Abigail Jacobs felt them out there, lurking among the trees in the endless night of Salem's Northern Woods. The chill of the grave flowed from their presence and froze her teenage flesh so deeply her bones ached.

Abigail's lantern glowed in the darkness like a lonesome star in a black and barren universe. A small iron charm forged in the shape of an ancient rune trembled in her outstretched hand. The metal was cold in her palm as she grasped it tight. She held it aloft, but it gave her a little comfort. She had been preparing for this night for months, steeling her courage against the horrors she would encounter. Now, the overwhelming malevolence of the spirits in the woods terrified her to the core. Every instinct screamed at her to turn around, to run back the way she had come and leave this place before its dark inhabitants tore her to pieces and warmed themselves with her blood.

Still, she pressed on.

The darkness was smothering, snaking around Abigail as if it meant to steal the light from her lantern. Her jaw hurt from clenching. How long had it been since she had crossed the threshold of this nightmare forest? It couldn't have been more than fifteen minutes, but it seemed like long and harrowing hours.

There had been a stiff and chilly wind beyond the borders of these woods, but in here, deep within the trees and their unseen horrors, nothing moved. The air was deathly still around her. There was no breeze to flutter the honey-blonde strands straying from Abigail's braided hair; no nocturnal music from the forest creatures to keep her company. *Lifeless* was the only word Abigail could think of to describe her surroundings. There was only a vast and empty silence and the awful awareness of undead eyes upon her, coveting her blood, waiting for when she would let down her guard.

*Your mother walked this same path,* Abigail reminded herself. *She did it for you...*

Abigail shuddered beneath her heavy pelisse and cloak as she ventured deeper and deeper into the black heart of this terrible place. Her thoughts went to the kind man who took her in when she was orphaned seven years ago this very night. She had left Jonas Hobbes slumbering in their snug cottage as she slipped away in the middle of the night. Abigail thought of Jonas's daughter, Emily. The young girl who had been a sister to her was now still tucked in her bed. Jonas had given both girls all the comforts he could muster, but his greatest gift had been teaching them to read. Because of him, Abigail had grown to be intelligent and sharp-witted.

It wasn't too late to return to them. She could forget this perilous mission and head back home to a normal life.

No, that was never her home. And any chance of a normal life was stolen from her seven years ago. Her only hope of getting it back lay ahead, somewhere in these cursed woods.

The empty satchel Abigail had slung over her shoulder swished against her hip as she threaded her way through the forest. Despite her fear, there was an undercurrent of excitement pulsing beneath her skin that kept pushing her to put one foot in front of the other. The protective talisman was working—at least for now. She could feel the dead lusting for her flesh, yet they were powerless against her. But was there a limit to the charm's influence? How much longer would it last? How long before she found the place she sought?

A terrified scream rippled through the darkness.

Abigail froze where she stood. Her skin prickled with goosebumps. The cry bounced among the trees before being swallowed up by the darkness. She couldn't be sure, but she thought it came from somewhere behind her, somewhere close.

The panic-stricken cry came again.

It was a chilling sound, but it didn't come from the undead.

It was a young man's voice.

A voice Abigail recognized.

Her heart galloped in her chest as she rushed back the way she had come. The lantern's light swung crazily from side to side on its ring, flashing over the exposed roots and underbrush and the enormous bases of the tree trunks on either side of the path. Just beyond the reach of its pale glow, the dead stared back at Abigail with baleful eyes and gaping mouths.

A young man lay sprawled on his stomach across the ground ahead. He was kicking and thrashing with his legs. His fingers dredged trenches through the forest floor as he strained to drag himself free from some unseen assailant. His head swung up at Abigail's approach and his straw-like hair fell away from his face. The lantern's light fell upon his features and Abigail recognized the pale blue eyes staring back at her in wide-eyed terror.

"Duncan!" Abigail rushed toward him and gasped when she saw what he was struggling so frantically against.

A skeletal hand was wrapped tight around his ankle. Reaching up from beneath the earth, it was hauling on his leg as if it meant to drag him deep down into the dirt.

Another ghastly hand broke through the ground and seized Duncan's outstretched arm by the wrist. He winced and cried out as a freezing agony shot up his arm.

Abigail froze. This was *real*. The undead hands grasping at her friend weren't some imaginary horror her mind had conjured when she lay awake envisioning this night—this was *really happening*.

Duncan let out a strangled moan and Abigail sprang into action. She dashed to his side and cringed as she pressed her iron talisman against the ghastly hand that snared his ankle.

An unholy shriek erupted from deep beneath the ground. The fleshless fingers instantly released their deadly grip.

Suddenly free, Duncan scrambled to his feet and scurried to Abigail's side.

"Keep back!" Abigail's shout echoed endlessly through the living darkness of the forest. She thrust out the talisman, eyes darting everywhere, expecting a spectral assault at any moment. "Keep back, I say! He is under my protection!"

A shrill chorus of unearthly voices arose in response.

*Warm our graves… Warm our graves… Warm our graves…*

Abigail grabbed Duncan's hand and ran. They kept close together as they fled along the path, dashing through the impenetrable darkness. From the corner of her eye, Abigail caught fleeting glimpses of dark and shapeless beings hovering amidst the thick tree trunks. Terrified and shaken, neither teen spoke until they broke free of the trees and burst into a small hollow.

Abigail kept her talisman clenched tight in her fist as she swept her eyes around the small grove. She sensed they were safer here. The overpowering sense of malice that had flowed from the dead had dissipated. Moonlight spilled down upon her and Duncan. The skeletal branches of the ring of trees twisted toward the night sky as if the teens stood at the center of an immense bowl of thorns.

Abigail's wintry eyes blazed with fury as she whirled on Duncan. "What are you doing here?"

"I—I was worried about you…" Duncan stammered.

"Worried? So you followed me? *Here?*"

"No, I…"

"You *what*, Duncan?"

Duncan opened his mouth to say something in his own defense, but thought better of it. He knew his willful friend well enough not to test her temper.

Duncan had grown to be a handsome young man since fate had thrown him and Abigail together as children. He now had high cheekbones and a tapered chin, but was not tall. At seventeen, he was two years older than Abigail and stood a head higher. His body was slim and his fingers long. Dead leaves and dirt still clung to his dusty overcoat. The bony claws of his undead attackers had shredded the stocking and breeches of one leg below his knee.

"You haven't been yourself for months, Abby," Duncan said when he pried his tongue free. "Not since…"

His voice trailed off again. Abigail knew he was thinking about that day in August.

It was a breezy afternoon, and they had been walking together in the meadow south of Mill Pond when Abigail surprised him with a kiss. It was an impulse, and she didn't know why she did it. Curiosity, most likely. Duncan was the only boy in Salem who talked to her—the only one who didn't *fear* her. The kiss was meant to last only a moment. But then something else happened, something that roused her to slip her tongue past his lips and into his mouth.

He stiffened with surprise, his wiry frame going rigid against hers as she pressed her small breasts into his chest. Then their tongues were dancing like sparrows flitting through the air, and she was running a hand through his hair as she pulled him down among the wildflowers. The syrupy scent of milkweed and lupins filled the air as she took his fingers and brought them beneath her muslin shift to her nipple. Her other hand fumbled at his breeches and slipped below his waistband.

"Not here," he whispered with little conviction or resolve.

"Yesss…" She moaned breathlessly into his ear as she hiked her shift up above her knees and mounted him. He was hard and ready as she guided him inside her and she felt a swift prick of pain from between her legs. Sweat trickled down the nape of her neck and dripped between her thin shoulder blades as she ground her hips into him. Soon, a shuddering warmth enveloped her, more blissful than the summer heat.

When it was over, they had lain there together on their backs, flushed and sweaty in the meadow. Duncan's breaths were quick and shuddering and Abigail felt no regret for what they had done. It had been her choice; exactly what she had wanted, whether she had known it or not. She didn't have any strong feelings for Duncan—and certainly no desire for marriage—but she trusted the young man more than anyone she had met since losing her parents. They shared a bond only the other survivors of that harrowing All Hallows' Eve could understand.

As they lay side-by-side in thunderstruck silence, Abigail stared up at the clouds and saw amorphous forms drifting across the summer sky. There was a schooner and a raven with wings outstretched and a howling wolf. And then Abigail saw something that froze her blood despite the humid summer air.

High above, the vaporous figure of a veiled woman glared down at her.

Abigail knew it was her imagination, but another cloud took on the same shape. Before long, she saw the same dreadful image everywhere she looked.

Soon after that day, Abigail began planning this night.

"You've been distant, Abby," Duncan now went on. The cold moonlight painted his thin face silver as he gazed at her in the grove. "I know you've been visiting grandfather's library when I'm not around. I don't know what you've been looking for— perhaps nothing—but 'tis as if you've been avoiding me. 'Tis as if… as if what we did was a mistake."

Abigail frowned. She *had* been avoiding Duncan, but not for the reasons he suspected. She required privacy for her research. Duncan would try to interfere in her plans, and she couldn't risk him discovering what she was up to.

Duncan's tongue stuck to the roof of his mouth, and he fell quiet for a moment. He cast a wary look around at the impenetrable gloom of the surrounding forest before changing the subject. "Does Jonas know you've—"

"Jonas is not my father," Abigail snapped. "And I don't require his permission to come and go as I please."

Duncan was going to say something more, but Abigail was already walking away.

"Wait!" He hustled across the hollow toward where the path picked up on the other side. "Where are you going?"

Abigail ignored his question. "Stay close if you insist on following me."

The path snaked through the trees like a twisting black stream. Duncan trailed behind as Abigail led the way with the lantern held high before her. Her strides were brisk and purposeful and almost masculine in their length.

"Those things back there… they were the spirits of those hanged during the witch trials, weren't they?" Duncan whispered as they went. "The villagers never buried their bodies; they left the corpses here to rot and they've haunted the woods of Gallows Hill ever since."

Abigail murmured an affirmative. One thing Duncan hadn't grown out of was his precociousness. He still preferred his grandfather's vast collection of books and maps to the rough-and-tumble games of other boys.

"And that charm…" Duncan gave a curious nod at the iron rune Abigail still held aloft.

"The talisman given to my mother the night of her death."

"I… I thought it was lost," Duncan remarked.

"I found it that night in the dirt on Gallows Hill. Since then, I have kept it a secret. Waiting…"

Duncan waited for her to go on, but she fell silent. "Waiting for what, Abby?"

Abigail drew to a sudden halt, and Duncan almost ran into her. He followed her gaze into the gloom and sucked in a sharp breath.

A ruined cabin loomed like a misshapen creature in the darkness ahead.

It was a crooked, single-story cottage shrouded beneath the claw-like boughs of the ancient trees. Thick tendrils of vines and ivy twisted up from the ground and enveloped the rotting timber frame like the tentacles of a kraken wrapped around a doomed ship. Large field-stones had fallen from the crumbling chimney and now lay strewn across the ground like ancient headstones. Green moss covered the cabin's warped roof and there were jagged holes exposed among the shingles. One side of the section that extended over the porch had collapsed, its tilted wreckage obscuring one of the two dingy windows that flanked the front door.

A door that stood wide open, an invitation into the yawning darkness within.

Duncan gaped at the forbidding structure. "Is that—"

"The home of Sarah Bridges," said Abigail. "The witch of Gallows Hill. The woman your grandfather helped murder on the town Common."

A stricken look crossed Duncan's boyish face. "'Twas a delusion of hysteria. I make no excuses for what Grandfather did, but he—"

"Come on…" Abigail headed for the cabin.

Three steps led up from the mud to the slanted porch. The planks creaked and flexed beneath Abigail's wary tread. She kept her footsteps light, certain her foot would break through the wood and snare her ankle. When she had mounted the porch, she motioned for Duncan to join her.

"Abby, we can't go in there." He kept his voice low, as if there was something frightening about the decaying cottage he might awaken if he spoke too loudly.

Abigail put a finger to her lips to hush him and gave him another impatient wave. She turned for the door and hesitated, her resolve faltering at the threshold. What terrors awaited her within that pooling darkness? But she hadn't risked her life in this accursed forest, only to turn back now.

With her heart pounding in her ears, Abigail crept through the door and let her lantern's light chase back the shadows of the cabin's interior.

Inside, there was nothing but silence. The large room was the shambled scene of a violent struggle. The floor was littered with shattered glass. Abigail surmised they were the remnants of bottles and jars the superstitious mob had smashed when they toppled the shelves from against the walls. The rare and macabre contents that had been Sarah Bridges' spell components were now strewn about the warped floorboards.

Ancient books lay scattered about, their brittle pages torn from their spines and shredded. A beam of moonlight streamed through a sizable hole where the roof had rotted through. Its pallid light cut through the darkness like a steel blade.

A pile of what looked to be charred bones sat heaped within the giant stone fireplace. A large oaken table stood near the hearth, the scarred wood stained with old blood. Animal skulls and the wax remains of dead candles cluttered its surface. In their midst sat a large bone-handled dagger and a book with deep crimson binding.

Abigail's heart leapt at the sight of the volume and a faint pink flush of excitement rose to her cheeks. "'Tis exactly as they left it the night the mob came for her. No one has stepped foot here in seven years."

The foul reek of rot and mildew filled her nose as she waded further into the gloom toward the large table and set the lantern down upon its surface. The surrounding room smelled sodden and green, like a stagnant pond.

"Abby… why have you come here?" Duncan glanced around at the heavy shadows in the corners. He searched for signs of movement, any warning of something horrific about to lunge out at them. "What do you hope to find?"

"What do you know of Sarah Bridges?" Abigail asked in return. She let her gaze wander over the scattering of arcane artifacts. Some were hideous; others were curious and lovely.

Duncan drew a breath and puffed it out with his cheeks. "The witch hysteria might have abated in the decades after the trials, but Salem's fearful superstitions endured. Sarah Bridges would have been a toddler when the townsfolk came for her family. There were rumors about them, dreadful tales of sacrifice and body-snatching and black magic. In years past, the Bridges family would have been charged and hanged, but the people of Salem were now contented to see them banished. Driven from their homestead and with nowhere else to turn, they sought refuge here in the haunted woods of Gallows Hill, where no one would dare come looking for them again. Years passed. Most assumed the Bridges family had died out here until the night Sarah Bridges returned to Salem, warning of the return of Rebecca Hale's vengeful spirit."

Abigail nodded, her eyes glittering in the lantern's light. "Seven years ago, on this very night, the spirits of Hale and her dead children returned to Salem to seek vengeance on the families who hanged them in secret during the witch trials. My mother died on Gallows Hill that night, Duncan… and we did not find her body. What if she becomes like them? A restless spirit cursed to roam alone for eternity somewhere between this world and the next?" Abigail's lips pressed into a grim line. "I won't let that happen—not to her."

Duncan gave her a wary look. "How do you intend to stop it?"

"With this." Abigail let her gaze settle on the crimson book sitting on the table before her.

There was a tremor in Abigail's hands as she reached for the ancient tome and laid her palms on the pentagram tooled into the blood-red leather. A strange sort of heat kissed her fingertips. She thought it came from the lantern, but it was too far away. No, the welcoming heat was emanating from the book itself.

Abigail understood why this book survived the mob that had come for Sarah Bridges when they had destroyed so many others. They would have thought this dreaded tome to be cursed.

Abigail opened the cover gingerly. Within were pages upon pages of arcane diagrams and spells, many written in indecipherable text and long-dead languages that Abigail didn't recognize. As she walked her fingers through the brittle parchment, she noticed the languages and handwriting changing over time.

Generations of witches had possessed this grimoire. And now it had come to her; centuries of arcane knowledge beneath her very fingertips.

An ecstatic tingle rippled through Abigail from her fingertips to her breast. She had felt powerless all her life. As a young girl, she could not dissuade her father from leaving on his ill-fated trip from Boston to Salem, a failure that led to deadly consequences. She had been helpless in stopping the vengeful spirit of Rebecca Hale from snatching her from her bed on that terrible All Hallows' Eve and possessing her youthful body as her own. And she couldn't prevent the death of her mother, who had sacrificed herself so that Abigail might live.

Now, Abigail could almost hear the spell-book whispering its promise of untold power. She hadn't been honest with Duncan about her motivations for coming to this dreadful place. There was another reason she had braved the perils of the haunted woods to find the home of Sarah Bridges, one she didn't dare admit to anyone: she had no intention of merely freeing her mother's spirit.

Abigail meant to bring her mother back.

And this Book of Shadows would teach her how.

"Abby, you can't seriously be thinking about practicing witchcraft." Duncan's face was aghast even as he remained ignorant of her true intentions.

"Why shouldn't I be? You know as well as I what they whisper about me in town. You've seen the sideways looks, the fearful glances. I am the only living descendant of Rebecca Hale, a woman so wicked the Devil himself freed her from Hell. The townsfolk already believe I'm a witch. Why shouldn't I embrace it? Witchcraft is in my blood. This book and the secrets it holds; these are my birthright. And if there is one thing I learned that night seven years ago, 'tis there is power in darkness."

"Abby—"

"There is no place for me in Salem, Duncan. And there never will be. What else am I expected to do?"

"You can marry me."

Abigail glared at him.

"Not now, of course," Duncan added hastily. "But someday soon, when you are ready."

"Marry you? Is it that simple for you? Will that solve everything?" There was an icy edge in Abigail's tone. "I have no desire to be married, Duncan. Not to you nor to any man. If you don't know that about me, then you have no business asking."

Duncan flinched a little and Abigail knew she had wounded him, but she didn't care. Better he should hurt now than waste his time clinging to false hope. Now that she had found Sarah Bridges' spell-book, the path ahead was a dark one that she must walk alone. Despite what had happened between them, Duncan would only hurt more if he didn't forget about her now.

Abigail avoided Duncan's gaze as she closed the cover on the Book of Shadows and slipped it into the satchel slung across her shoulder. She had found what she came for; it was time to leave.

The cabin shuddered.

Abigail and Duncan locked eyes as an eerie creaking filled the room, as if a powerful gust buffeted the ramshackle cottage. But that was impossible. No wind penetrated the thick forest.

The pair stared at each other, fear gnawing at their insides.

That's when the tapping began.

It came from outside, a gentle knocking against the timber wall. Not an insistent rap, but a soft and tentative patter. It went on a heartbeat longer. Then fell quiet.

A nerve-straining silence filled the room. Abigail and Duncan stood rooted to the floor, every muscle tense and quivering with fright.

Something was out there. What was it? And was it trying to get in?

There it was again!

Abigail jolted at the sound. It was stronger, more forceful. The knocking was higher up the wall and slightly to the left.

*Tap… Tap… Tap…*

The patter shifted once more, creeping further upward toward the roof. A sickening dread gripped Abigail's insides as she traced its slow movement with her eyes. The strange sound wasn't that of something probing the outside wall.

It was the sound of something *climbing*.

*Tap… Tap… Tap…*

The footsteps—yes, that's what they were—reached the roof. A fresh wave of fear washed over Abigail. The ceiling's rotting beams groaned under the weight of whatever was up there.

The thing moved sideways. There was the cracking and splintering of brittle shingles and a harsh scraping as they slid away underfoot.

A dark shape eclipsed the moonlight beaming through the hole in the roof.

Abigail stifled a cry and held her breath. Her eyes darted to the bloodstained dagger on the table, but she didn't dare reach for it. She tried to swallow, but the spit had dried up in her mouth. She felt Duncan's terrified eyes on her and prayed he wouldn't make a move.

The thing on the roof went still.

Seconds ticked by. Abigail's blood pounded in her temples. Did the thing know they were there? Was it staring down at them through the jagged hole above?

The air exploded with shards of glass as a window burst inward. This time, Abigail couldn't bite back her scream.

Fingers poked through the gaping hole in the window-frame. A bony hand followed, putrid and livid with decay, and then a rotting arm.

Abigail's breath was sucked out of her. Her entire body shook as more of the monstrous thing appeared in the window and dragged itself through. It tumbled through the dim light at the limits of the lantern's pale radius and crouched on the floor. The ghastly thing's head swiveled around and its long black hair fell away from its decomposing face. Its corpse-like skin stretched tight across its skull and its eye sockets were hollow holes.

The thing on the roof dropped through the hole and hit the floorboards. The planks rattled beneath it as it rose in the murky shadows.

A warm hand clamped onto Abigail's wrist, and she was being yanked sideways across the room. Duncan's grip on her was viselike as he hauled her toward the open door, desperate to escape the hideous monstrosities invading the cabin.

A third walking corpse lurched from the porch into the door frame.

Duncan didn't have time to stop. The thing's rotting hand swung up and gripped him by the throat. His face turned a horrible shade of scarlet, and a high-pitched wheeze rasped through his strangled windpipe. Then he was sailing across the room, hurled backward with inhuman strength. His skull struck the stone of the fireplace with a wet smack and his head whipped forward on his neck as he crumpled in a heap across the cold hearth.

Abigail tried to scream, but her throat closed up. Only a strangled moan came out. Seized by a paralyzing terror, she had a wild urge to close her eyes. She had the foolish idea that if she couldn't see these unholy abominations, they would somehow cease to exist. It occurred to her then that she knew what these walking abominations were.

There were three of them, just like the dead members of Sarah Bridges' family.

These were their reanimated corpses.

And they protected the Book of Shadows.

Chills convulsed Abigail's lithe frame as she retreated. The backs of her thighs banged into the heavy table. The three corpses took up positions around her like the points of a triangle.

Abigail noticed they lingered just beyond the reach of the lantern's light, their decomposing faces glowing a ghostly white in the darkness. The lantern's flame repelled them.

By some unspoken signal, their hideous mouths all fell open at the same time. Hollow voices issued from their motionless jaws as if something *else* lived inside their decaying carcasses.

*"We know why you have come…"* the terrible voices intoned in unison. They were bottomless and gravelly, as if echoing up from the depths of Hell. *"Your mother is here with us, beyond the Veil…"*

An electric jolt shot through Abigail like a lightning strike.

How could these ghastly creatures know about her mother?

Unless…

Unless there was truth in what they were saying.

"*She may yet return to you,*" the dreadful chorus said as one, the voices spilling out of the gaping holes of the corpses' mouths. "*Tonight, when the Veil is at its thinnest…*"

Abigail's heart quickened in her chest. All of her rational thoughts told her this was madness. But a desperate part of her scratched away at her convictions. She had no reason to trust these monstrous creatures. But what if it were possible? What if she could bring her mother back tonight?

"How?" The word shook through her Abigail's lips. "What must I do?"

All three corpses raised their arms at once and pointed their rotting fingers at Duncan's lifeless body.

"*Blood…*"

A chill ran through Abigail's veins as she realized what they were asking. She felt a terrible tightness in her chest and her throat constricted so tightly she struggled to draw a breath. "No… I can't…"

"*Your mother must have blood to live anew…*"

Abigail turned her gaze to where Duncan lay sprawled across the floor. A crimson pool was collecting beneath his head. It didn't seem possible. The boy she had grown up with—the young man she had shared such intimacy with—couldn't have come to such a sudden end. But the sound of his skull smacking against the hard stone still echoed in her memory.

Abigail willed herself to think clearly. Her mind was drowning in fear and adrenaline. The only things that surfaced were fragmented memories of her mother alive. Many were already being forgotten by the passing of years. But Abigail still remembered her mother's tenderness. She clung to the echo of her mother's last words to her as she had closed the bedroom door that fateful All Hallows' Eve: *You are all the magic I have ever known…*

Abigail would give anything to feel the comforting warmth of that touch again; to have her mother's gentle voice chase away the nightmares that had haunted her for almost a decade. Duncan was already dead… and Abigail had waited so very long to see her mother again. She had already been on the precipice of believing it was possible. It took little to push her over.

Abigail reached for the dagger on the table. The bone hilt was cold to the touch, and she shuddered as she wrapped her palm around it.

Just as she had done that day in August, Abigail knelt and straddled her friend. She had walked into that meadow a girl and left as a woman, one who was prepared to sacrifice anything to get what she wanted. She couldn't be certain that Duncan was already dead, but a dark part of her didn't *want* to know, not if it meant losing her one opportunity to return her mother from beyond the Veil. The sacrifice had to be made tonight.

It had to be done now.

A horrible nausea roiled Abigail's stomach, but she still raised the knife into the air. Her hand quivered as she readied to strike. Fear surged through her, a gut-wrenching terror such as she had never known. There was no returning from the terrible act she was about to commit. She drew a deep and trembling breath, trying to still her racing heart. One powerful thrust to Duncan's chest and this would all be over. His senseless death would be redeemed. His blood would return her mother from beyond the Veil and reunite them at long last.

The corpses stared at her from the corners of the room, waiting for Abigail to strip the flesh from his bones.

She clenched the dagger's hilt.

And froze.

Duncan's chest moved.

It was the faintest of flutters, but it was still a breath.

He was still alive.

Abigail's hand stiffened in the air. She swept her gaze around at the living corpses surrounding her. They had lied to her and almost made her do the unthinkable. The veil of grief and hope that had blinded her fell from her eyes. She saw these beings for what they were.

Evil.

Just like the evil that possessed her as a girl…

That stole her childhood…

That killed her mother…

Abigail's blood simmered with a rage so fierce it was staggering. She felt consumed by a burning black hatred. Her palm clenched tight around the dagger. These abominations had exploited her rawest wounds. They had tempted her into murdering her one genuine friend. She would make them pay; she would end their time on this earth forever.

She would end them *all*.

In one swift motion, Abigail whirled around, snatched the lantern from the table, and hurled it at the nearest corpse. The glass chimney shattered, soaking the thing with oil that ignited instantly. Flames shot up and engulfed the monster in their searing heat.

The corpse reeled backward, flailing at itself. The flames cast a brilliant orange glow across the walls.

Abigail sensed the second corpse lurching for her from behind. Its bony fingers brushed her shoulder just as she spun around and sliced the dagger through the air. The blade cleaved through the rotting flesh of the corpse's throat. Supported only by its spine, its moldering head tilted hideously to one side, but the monster didn't relent in its advance.

Abigail stumbled backward. Her feet got tangled beneath her and she hit the floor hard.

The corpse fell on her, clawing at her flesh with its broken nails. Abigail screamed and struggled to fight it off. The dagger was trapped between them. She twisted it in her grip and thrust it upward. The blade speared into the corpse's gut and split it open. Decomposing innards spilled over Abigail as she thrashed beneath it. Scorching bile leapt into her throat. With a desperate effort, she shoved the weakened creature off and scrambled away.

Duncan had somehow staggered up to one knee during the struggle. Blood still trickled down the nape of his neck and soaked his collar as Abigail rushed to his side and propelled him to his feet.

"Come on!" She shoved him toward the door.

The entire room was ablaze now. The flames leapt up the timber walls to the ancient ceiling. Smoke choked the air.

Duncan stumbled forward on wobbly legs and pitched out onto the porch with Abigail right behind him, her eyes and throat burning

One corpse came shambling from the open door. Flames engulfed it, a walking torch with arms outstretched.

Abigail felt the blistering heat as it barreled toward her. She swung the dagger through the air. The fire licked her skin as she plunged the blade into the side of the corpse's head. She jerked her hand back. The creature dropped to the ground with the dagger still stuck in its temple. Flames consumed its bone handle.

Abigail spun around. There was movement inside the inferno of the cottage. Two more black silhouettes loomed in the doorframe, coming for them. Abigail stole a glance at Duncan. His face was ashen, his eyes glassy and unfocused. He could barely remain upright without her support and was in no shape to run.

She had only two options: leave him behind or stay and fight. But with what?

Without warning, there was a teeth-rattling roar. The entire roof of the cottage came crashing down, devoured by flames. For a fleeting instant, Abigail saw the walking corpses scuttling through the doorway and then they were crushed beneath the immense weight of the burning wreckage. A billowing cloud of smoke and sparks spiraled high into the night air.

The heat of the inferno pressed against Abigail's back as she hooked an arm around Duncan. Together, they staggered away from the blazing ruins of the cabin. Her thoughts strayed back to those trembling moments when she had straddled her friend's motionless body and almost plunged the knife into his chest. She hadn't known he was still alive, but she wanted so badly to be reunited with her mother that a dark part of her had actually hoped he was dead. Given a few more moments, she might have killed him, regardless.

It was a truth so shamefully shocking it filled her with revulsion. She pushed it down deep, never to be spoken of again.

Instead, Abigail let the elation of her victory wash over her. Something had awakened in her, a lust for vengeance that had simmered in her veins for seven years. She had found release in putting an end to monsters like the Bridges family. For the first time since the night her parents died, she felt some of the rage and grief she carried had lifted. It might prove only a fleeting solace, but it was one she would yearn for over and over. Others could be spared her parents' fate. They could be saved from evil —and *she* could be the one to do it.

Abigail felt the weight of the magical tome in the satchel swinging against her hip. Even if it took years, working in secret while she studied the forbidden, she would unlock the mysteries of the Book of Shadows and bring her mother back to her.

Until then, she would rid the world of every evil bastard she came across.

*Author's Note*

This companion story to the *Book of Shadows* novels takes place between *The Suicide Lake* and *The Wolf Society*, but can be enjoyed at any time.

## The Haunting of Siren's Inn

The woman's screams pierced the silence from the floor above and rattled the old bones of the Siren's Inn.

Abigail Jacobs dashed up the broad steps of the grand switchback staircase two-at-a-time. She reached the third floor just as the terror-stricken woman came streaking down the darkened hallway toward her. They collided, and Abigail caught her in her arms. The impact rocked her back on her heels and they both came perilously close to pitching backward over the stairs before Abigail regained her balance.

The young woman buried her face in the shoulder of Abigail's Spencer jacket and sobbed. "Please, please, please…"

"What is it? What happened?" Abigail felt the woman's heart beating wildly through her flannel nightgown.

"There is a man in my room! He… *Oh God*…" The woman's voice cracked. "He was killing Philip!"

Abigail threw a glance into the silent gloom stretching out before her. There were no candles lit at this late hour. Heavy shadows obscured the far limits of the inn's oak-paneled corridor. Abigail could make out the black portal of an open door at the end of the hall.

*Room Nine…*

Abigail peered deeper into the darkness.

Something moved within the doorway; a shadow within the shadows.

"Hurry, come with me," Abigail said with an uneasy edge in her voice.

She ushered the woman down the stairs, casting anxious glances over her shoulder as they went. The killer's looming shape was certain to appear over the third-floor balustrade at any moment. Abigail's hand clamped tight on the elegant oak banister. She listened nervously for the sound of heavy footsteps thumping from the shadowy room at the end of the hall.

There was nothing but an ominous silence on the floor above.

Abigail glanced back as they reached the half-landing. "What is your name?"

"Mason," the woman replied between sniffles. Her chestnut hair was a tousled mess and her hazel eyes were watery and red. Her pretty face was dreadfully pale and her round cheeks were ruddy with tears. "Bridget Mason."

"Bridget, my name is Abigail Jacobs. I'm going to help you."

Abigail's thirteen-year-old daughter, Anna, appeared at the foot of the stairs on the second floor and peered up at them. She and her mother were identical in almost every feature, from their full lips to their teardrop-shaped noses and their wintry blue eyes. The one exception was their hair: Abigail's was a flowing honey-blonde, but her daughter's was as black as a raven's wing. Though it was past midnight, Anna wore in a woolen tunic suited for travel, not bedclothes.

"Anna, wake the innkeeper!" Abigail instructed. "Have him fetch the constable. Go quickly!"

Anna nodded and raced down the stairs, disappearing out of sight around a corner in the dim foyer below.

"No!" Without warning, Bridget spun on her heels and started back up the steps. "We can't wait! Philip is dying inside that room!"

"Bridget! Don't go up there!" Abigail reached for her, but Bridget was already pounding up toward the third floor again.

Abigail clambered up after her, the sturdy oaken treads creaking beneath her feet. She reached the top in time to see Bridget melt into the darkness of the third-floor hallway. Abigail followed. Her footsteps were far too loud in the silence and her heart pounded with dread. What would they discover in the room? Her skin tingled, and she readied herself for a bloody confrontation as Bridget halted at the open door to Room Nine.

In the darkness, there was nothing but neatly arranged furniture and a four-post bed.

Bridget stared at the undisturbed bedsheets in confusion. "I… I don't understand… What happened here? Where is Philip? His blood was all over the floor…" She marched into the room and threw open the curtains.

Snow blasted through the darkness outside and a ferocious wind rattled the leaded windowpanes. A vicious Nor'easter was whipping through the seaside fishing village of Gloucester.

The Siren's Inn stood on the south side of Front Street, on the water overlooking the long wharves of Harbor Cove. Any other night, Room Nine would have afforded a splendid view of the cove and Rocky Neck. Now, nothing of the harbor or cove was visible now. The world beyond the bedroom window ended in a billowing curtain of white. Now and then there was the booming thunder of windblown waves crashing against the wharves. The constant *bang! bang! bang!* of a loose shutter on a neighboring building was the only other sign that anything else existed out in the storm.

Bridget spun from the window. Her eyes darted around the dusky room, searching for any clue to suggest she wasn't losing her mind. There was a pair of nightstands and a dresser, but nothing else; no evidence of a struggle, let alone a grisly murder.

"I know what I saw," Bridget insisted. "The man was right *here*. He… he must have taken Philip somewhere."

"I believe you," Abigail said. "The killer could be anywhere in this building. We are the inn's only guests and we'll freeze to death if we venture out in that storm. We're trapped here and the safest place for us is behind locked doors. Please come back to my room. Let's wait for help to arrive."

Bridget's thin brows furrowed. She seemed about to resist again until her thin shoulders slumped in defeat. With a last glance around, she followed Abigail into the corridor and back toward the stairs.

They reached the second floor just as Anna came racing back up the steps to meet them. The ringlets of her black hair spilled like ink around her face, and her mesmerizing blue eyes leapt as she panted for air. "The innkeep has gone for the constable, but it may be some time in this storm. He said it would be best if we remained in our room until they return."

With Bridget trailing behind as they hustled down the corridor, Abigail leaned close to Anna and murmured so that only her daughter would hear. "She doesn't know what happened in this inn."

"We should tell her the truth," Anna whispered.

Abigail shook her head. "No, she can't leave this place. Not yet. We need her here, with us."

"Need her for what?" Then it dawned on Anna. "You want to use her as bait?"

The glint in Abigail's frosty blue eyes was the only answer her daughter needed.

The Siren's Inn was a seaside retreat built to attract wealthy summer tourists who came from Boston to enjoy coastal walks and bathe at the beach stretching westward from nearby Fort Defiance. The inn boasted a luxurious sitting room and modern dining. Twelve rooms were divided equally between the two upper floors.

The room Abigail shared with Anna was at the end of the second-floor hallway, directly beneath Room Nine. As advertised, it was large and well-appointed. A comfortable four-poster occupied most of the space, flanked on either side by nightstands upon which candles now burned. The orange glow of the flames threw shadows dancing around the room and filled the air with the syrupy scent of beeswax. The curtains were open, revealing the same view of the storm-ravaged harbor as the floor above. A walnut chest of drawers stood against the wall opposite the bed. Abigail's travel valise sat atop it, along with a bulky burlap sack.

No sooner had she bolted the bedroom door behind them than Anna threw open the valise and snatched a large glass flask from within. She darted back to the door and poured a mound of dirt along the threshold.

Bridget eyed her. "What is that?"

"Graveyard dust," Anna replied. "It's consecrated. Spirits can't cross over it."

"Spirits?" Bridget stared at the girl like she hadn't heard correctly.

"Tell me what happened, Bridget," Abigail interjected.

A shudder wracked Bridget's shoulders and her white nightgown quivered on her slender frame. "The man was standing at the foot of the bed when I awoke. He… he was just *staring* at us. I don't know how he got into the room or how long he had been there, watching us as we slept. I screamed when I saw him and Philip leapt from the bed. But the man, he… he slashed at Philip with a knife. I saw the blood spilling from his stomach and I ran. God help me, I ran and left him there to die!"

Bridget's face crumpled with anguish and she buried it in her hands.

Across the room from each other, Abigail and Anna exchanged grave looks.

"Can you tell me about this man?" Abigail prodded. "What did he look—"

There was an eerie creak on the floor above.

The trio froze at the sound. It would be easy to imagine it resulted from the howling storm pummeling the inn. But they knew what they had heard.

A footstep.

"It's him." Bridget's hands shook as she inched away from the door.

Another footstep overhead. The unmistakable *thump* of a heavy boot. Loud. Menacing.

Abigail sprang to the valise and produced a compact flintlock. Bridget gawked at the pistol as Abigail set to loading it.

They could hear the muffled footsteps descending the

staircase now, thumping their way inexorably down toward the second floor.

Toward *them*.

"Get behind me, Anna," Abigail whispered.

Anna did as she was told, scurrying between her mother and Bridget.

*Thump… Thump… Thump…*

"Oh God, he's coming this way." Bridget whimpered and pressed herself against the far wall, flinching with each booming step.

Abigail kept her ears pricked to track the footsteps as they progressed down the corridor. They were getting closer now. She reached beneath the collar of her Spencer jacket for the leather cord she wore around her neck and tugged on the iron talisman she kept on her at all times. She clutched the rune-shaped charm with one hand and aimed the pistol at the door with the other.

*Thump… Thump… Thump…*

The footsteps halted just outside the room.

Bridget's heart clenched in her chest. Paralyzed with dread, her legs were nerveless pieces of kindling.

The doorknob squeaked. Slow, tentative. The knob turned just a little. The lock caught and the unnerving squeak became a rattle. Harder. More insistent. The door shook violently on its hinges.

An icy fingertip of fear brushed a line up Bridget's spine. Her terrified breaths came in shallow bursts as she shrank back against the windowsill. Some primal instinct told her whatever lurked beyond that door wasn't natural. It couldn't be.

The shaking stopped. Silence returned to the room and with it, a foreboding sense of menace.

A freezing chill slithered through the cracks around the door, as if someone had thrown open a window in the corridor.

Abigail took a steadying breath and let it out. She cocked the pistol and kept it trained on the door.

A strange groaning came from everywhere at once, as if the walls were straining under some incredible pressure being exerted on the other side.

Anna shot a nervous glance at her mother. Abigail's attention was still riveted on the door.

Cracks appeared in the plaster walls as the moment stretched on. The floor beneath their feet creaked like the deck of a ship rocking from side-to-side on rough seas. A rusty screeching filled the room. The iron nailheads appeared from the floorboards. They rose from the pinewood as if they were being pried loose by some invisible force.

Anna stared at the floor beneath her as more of the planks buckled and twisted under their feet. One sprang up beneath the door.

Just enough to scatter the graveyard dust heaped along the threshold.

Abigail's heart lurched into her throat. It all happened too quickly; she saw their protection breaking and was powerless to stop it.

The bedroom door slammed wide open.

An immense man stood on the other side. He was well over six feet in height and thickly muscled. His long, dark hair hung in wet strings over his bearded face, as if he had just come in from weathering the raging storm outside. He dressed like a fisherman with heavy, knee-high boots over his dark cloth breeches and a heavy woolen greatcoat. The wide collar was open and the linen shirt he wore beneath his coat clung to his barrel chest and hardened stomach. His skin was terribly pale, so white it seemed translucent and revealed the spiderwebs of blue veins beneath. Worst of all were the man's eyes. They were corpse-white and devoid of all color. No irises, no pupils; just hideous blank voids as opaque as the endless snow.

Clenched in the man's big right hand was a bone-handled gutting knife.

Bridget screamed as the man barreled through the door, his massive figure filling the frame. With his baleful eyes fixed on Bridget, his glare seemed to pass right through Abigail and Anna as if they weren't present and standing in his way.

Bridget moaned and slid sideways across the wall as if the extra few inches of distance might somehow save her.

In the same instant, Abigail lunged and thrust out her iron talisman.

The big man skidded to a halt where he stood and recoiled, hissing at her like a furious serpent and glaring with his dreadful eyes.

Abigail aimed the pistol at his face and fired.

The gun roared with a dazzling spray of sparks. Instead of blowing the man's skull apart and blasting a grisly spray of brains against the wall, the juggernaut's figure exploded into tendrils of white mist before vanishing into the air.

An uneasy silence filled the room as the echo of the gun-blast still thundered in their ears. The acrid stench of gun smoke hung thick around them.

Bridget blinked. "What happened? Where did he go?"

Abigail glanced at her and reloaded the pistol. "Iron bullets forged from a cemetery gate. They can't kill him, but they can buy us some time."

Anna was heaping another mound of graveyard dust over the warped floorboards by the door. She stoppered the flask and looked at her mother. "Perhaps it's time we told her the truth, Mother?"

"The truth about what?" Bridget demanded. "What haven't you been telling me?"

Abigail frowned as she poured the pistol's powder. "Be quick about it."

Anna crossed the room and eased Bridget onto the edge of the bed. "Twenty-one years ago, a young man and his fiancé were on their way from Boston to be married in the man's hometown of Rockport. A Nor'easter much like this one obliged them to take shelter in this inn. Unbeknownst to them, a jilted lover of the young woman had followed them, determined to stop their marriage at all costs. The man's name was Judah Abbott, and he disemboweled the woman's fiancé before her eyes. He then strangled the woman in her bed before flinging himself to his death over the third floor balustrade. This all happened in Room Nine—*your* room, you understand? And every seven years on the anniversary of that bloody night, Judah's spirit returns to this inn to reenact his murderous deeds. This year, he has chosen you."

Bridget's mouth hung open as she glanced from Anna to Abigail. "That man was a ghost?"

Abigail nodded. "Had I not intervened at the right moment, he would have dragged you back to Room Nine and strangled you in your bed."

"What about Philip? Where has he gone?"

"He's dead," Anna replied.

A grief-stricken look darkened Bridget's pale face. She folded her arms over her nightgown and dipped forward slightly. Her lips moved but couldn't summon any words. She stared at Anna, eyes unfocused, until she gathered herself up and pushed herself from the wall. "I don't believe it. I'm going to get help myself."

"I'm afraid that is quite impossible," Abigail insisted. "He won't let you leave."

Bridget paused at the closed door.

"Your only hope is to help us."

Bridget turned around. "Help you do what?"

"Banish Judah's spirit before he kills you."

Abigail ignored the distress blooming on Bridget's face and went to the dresser, where she untied the burlap sack. An unholy reek escaped into the room as she reached inside and produced a severed human hand. The flesh was livid and mottled with decay. A jagged stump of white bone protruded where the wrist should be.

Bridget gagged and covered her mouth with a palm. "Is that —"

"A dead man's hand? Yes."

"Is it his? Judah's?"

"No. This one is decidedly more fresh."

Bridget's nose wrinkled with disgust. "Where did it come

from?"

"A hanged man." From the same sack, Abigail produced a tallow candle and a rotted shred of fabric stained with something dark and rusty.

"What is that?" Bridget wasn't certain she wanted the answer.

"Judah's blood. Obtained from his grave at First Parish Burial Ground."

"His grave? You dug him up?"

"Not all of him," Anna quipped. "'Tis hard work, the ground being frozen hard this time of year."

"We have been preparing for this night for some time," Abigail added.

"Preparing? You knew this would happen?" Bridget's gaze darted from Abigail to Anna and back. "Who *are* you?"

"Someone who puts an end to such beings," Abigail replied.

Bridget glanced at Anna. "And you? Are you—"

"Her apprentice."

Bridget stared at Abigail, aghast. "How could you?"

Abigail shot her a scathing look. "A mother doesn't protect her child from evil by deceiving her into thinking it doesn't exist."

Abigail pressed the bloodstained scrap into the palm of the severed hand and curled the stiff fingers tight around the rotted cloth. Anna handed her a length of thorny vine from the burlap sack and Abigail wrapped it around the rotting hand, twisting the vine to keep the fingers balled into a fist. She then took the candle and squeezed it between the hand's curled middle and ring fingers so that the wick pointed upward, as if the severed hand were some macabre candlestick.

"We'll need fire," Abigail said.

"The embers are still burning in the sitting room," Anna suggested.

Abigail grabbed the pistol and started for the door. "We must hurry, we haven't much time."

The mound of graveyard dust scattered beneath their feet and left a trail of footprints as they left the room.

The length of the corridor lay in eerie silence. Though it was only the mournful moan of the wind, Bridget imagined she could hear the deserted inn itself drawing breath. Her mouth went dry and her heart hammered in her chest as they crept to the majestic staircase. She didn't dare look up, too terrified of seeing Judah Abbott's ghastly face staring back at her from over the third floor balustrade.

The stairs descended to the foyer, a grand area designed to wrap guests in the arms of luxury upon their arrival at the inn. Large windows of stained-leaded glass flanked the wide double-doors of the front entrance. Solid oak panelling covered the walls and a giant brass chandelier hung suspended from the soaring beamed ceiling. The candles were burning low now and cast a pale glow over the space.

Abigail led the way across the foyer to the inn's opulent lounge, an impressive sitting room of magnificent scale. Massive oak beams supported the coffered ceiling, and the walls featured bespoke cabinetry with leaded glass. Rows of leather-bound volumes stood behind the cabinet panes, along with a collection of marble busts and precise miniatures of masted sailing ships. Gilded frames hung between the candles of the wall sconces, displaying dramatic seascapes and portraits of Gloucester's intrepid pioneers and fishing captains.

A trio of cabriole sofas were arranged around an ornate coffee table at the center of the room. Set into the far wall opposite the entrance and surrounded by hammered copper was the room's massive fireplace. A glowing mound of coals still burned on the grate. Above the mantle, a large mirror afforded the room's guests a view of themselves surrounded by such splendid finery.

Abigail set the severed hand on the coffee table and laid a fresh log across the embers. She pumped the bellows and the burning coals leapt to life like the lidded eye of a demon. The dry log crackled and flames sprang up on the hearth.

Smoke twirled up the chimney as Abigail set the bellows aside and retrieved the dead man's hand. She lit the wick of the tallow candle protruding from between the fist's knuckles. The sickly reek of rendered fat filled the air.

Bridget wrinkled her nose on the side of the room near the darkened window. "I don't understand. How is that... that revolting *thing* supposed to defeat that evil creature?"

"The Hand of Glory is an ancient and powerful occult item," Abigail explained. "When presented to a person, it renders them motionless for a time. The same holds true for spirits such as Judah. While he remains held in thrall, we will summon a Familiar to drag him across the Veil where he belongs."

Bridget blinked. It was coming at her too fast. "A Familiar?"

"A spirit I have bound to my service. Now, please remain very still and silent, no matter what you witness here."

Abigail handed the pistol to Anna and clutched the lit Hand of Glory to her breast. She stood facing the fireplace, the flames bathing her in their warm radiance and casting flickering shadows across her face. A deep and foreboding silence settled on the room.

Bridget and Anna stood by and watched as Abigail closed her eyes and chanted in the serpentine language of magic.

*You are all going to die*, a dark voice whispered in Anna's head. A chill raced up her spine, and her blood turned to ice in her veins. It wasn't her own thoughts speaking to her; it was the haunting voice of a woman. She had heard it before, whispering to her on dark and lonely nights when her body ached from training under her mother's tutelage. But the voice had never been so clear, so *present*. It came to Anna like a breath escaping from a lonely tomb. A voice of smoke and ashes.

*The Hand of Glory will fail,* the voice rasped. *He is going to kill you all...*

Anna's insides twisted. She looked at her mother. Abigail's eyes were still closed, and she titled her head back as she invoked her Familiar to do her bidding.

Anna squirmed where she stood and bit the inside of her cheek as she wrestled with her misgivings. Somehow, she knew the voice in her head spoke the truth; Abigail was making a dreadful mistake.

"Mother, this isn't right." Anna's voice was strained. "This will not work."

Lost in the rapture of witchcraft, Abigail went on with her invocation.

"Mother!" Anna repeated, more forcefully now. "It will not work! He's too powerful!"

Without warning, Bridget let out a blood-curdling shriek.

They were no longer alone.

The spirit of Judah Abbott struck with preternatural speed. His bear-claw of a hand lashed out and snarled a fistful of Bridget's thick hair. Her eyelids distorted into round circles as he yanked hard and began dragging her from the room. She backpedalled, heels scrabbling across the waxed floor, struggling to keep the lumbering spirit from ripping the hair from her head by its roots. Her scalp was aflame, the searing pain shooting down her spine. The agony was so excruciating her vision dimmed, invaded by a swirling black fog. She struggled and fought to dispel it, clinging to consciousness, desperate to remain in this world among the living.

Abigail's invocation ceased. Her icy blue eyes flew open.

Above the fireplace mantle, a ghostly mist was gathering within the ornate mirror. The mist filled the gilded frame with swirling layers of white, as if its reflective surface was a window to some shadowy world. And then the mist pushed *through* the mirror into the sitting room.

Abigail gathered up the Hand of Glory and shielded the lit candle. The delicate flame flickered behind her palm as she darted across the room toward Judah's retreating figure.

"Anna, now!"

Anna raised the pistol and fired.

The gun roared. The bullet went wide of Judah's massive figure and blasted a splintered hole in the oak paneling. After years of relentless training, Anna's aim with a pistol was now deadly accurate. But she never intended this shot to hit the spirit, just catch his attention. Judah spun around—right toward Abigail.

She thrust out the Hand of Glory as if offering him a gift and the malevolent spirit froze where he stood. His terrible grip on Bridget's hair lost its strength and released. She squirmed free, gasping and gulping air as she scrambled away.

Across the room, the ghostly mist crawled through the air from the giant mirror. Judah stood immobilized against his will as Abigail's spectral Familiar engulfed him in a swirling cloud of white. Judah's corpse eyes flew wide. He threw back his head and let out an unearthly wail, thrashing as the mist dragged him back to the mirror.

And then they were gone.

An eerie stillness settled over the sitting room.

Anna's gaze went from the empty spot where the murderous spirit had been to her mother.

Abigail's chest heaved and her face was flushed, but her blue eyes glittered with exhilaration. Her plan had worked; Judah Abbott's spirit had been dragged across the Veil.

"No more of this!" Bridget's exclamation echoed through the empty inn. "I'm leaving now, storm be damned!"

"No, Bridget! Don't!" Abigail chased after her as Bridget marched into the foyer.

Bridget ignored her. She stormed to the double-doors, reached for the doorknob.

And her hand passed right through it.

Bridget went rigid, too shocked to move.

"We tried to tell you," Abigail said from across the foyer.

Bridget stared at her palm in fascinated horror. "What... What is happening?"

"Judah Abbott isn't the only spirit to return to the Siren's Inn on the anniversary of his death. You died that night, too, Bridget. *You* were the woman Judah strangled in her bed."

"What?" Bridget gaped at her. "That's ridiculous. I'm no ghost! I've never even been to Gloucester before! Were it not for this storm, we never would have—"

"What storm, Bridget?" Anna interrupted. "Look outside."

Bridget stared at the girl for a moment before swinging her

attention to the windows of the inn's entrance.

Moonlight spilled down from a clear winter sky. The reflected light of twinkling stars danced across the calm waters of the cove.

Bridget retreated from the windows in confusion. "But the snow… It… It was knee-high…"

"No," Abigail said gently. "There is no storm tonight. But there was a Nor'easter twenty-one years ago. Your death at Judah's hands froze you in time, Bridget. And every seven years he brings you back to kill you again."

Bridget shook her head. "You're lying! This isn't possible…"

"Look again." Abigail motioned toward the windows. "Do you see that windmill? The one atop the hill in the distance? It wasn't there when you arrived here in Gloucester, was it?"

Bridget stared out the window at the windmill spinning in the moonlight and gave the slightest shake of her head. "No." Her murmur was almost inaudible. "It wasn't there."

"They erected that mill in 1814," Abigail revealed. "Nine years *after* your death. Think hard, Bridget. The time has come to remember beyond the events of that terrible night. Where were you and Philip traveling when the storm forced you to shelter at this inn?"

"We… we were on our way to be…" Bridget's voice fell off a cliff. The forgotten past crashed over her and she realized what she was about to say.

"To be married," Abigail finished for her.

Bridget glanced about and gasped. For the first time in decades, she saw her surroundings clearly.

The grand foyer was now dark and cast in gloomy blue by the brilliant moonlight streaming through the windows. Cobwebs hung in ghostly wisps from the unlit chandelier, its brass surface now tarnished and covered in dust.

"This isn't possible…" Bridget marched from the foyer back to the sitting room. It now sat in brooding darkness. The fire still crackled on the grate, but the copper surround of the fireplace was dented and covered by a greenish patina. The paintings were gone and all the furniture had been removed, leaving the room nothing but four bare walls and cavernous shadows. A thick layer of dust blanketed the surfaces and floor, disturbed only by Abigail and Anna's footprints.

Bridget had left none.

"This... this place is abandoned," Bridget whispered with dawning understanding.

Abigail offered a sad smile. "They say 'tis haunted."

"By me."

Abigail nodded.

"But the innkeeper—"

"We told you only what you were ready to hear until you were prepared to accept the truth. The Siren's Inn hasn't seen an innkeep in many years. Not since the last unfortunate deaths."

Bridget's eyebrows knit together. "Deaths? Have I... Have I hurt anyone?"

Abigail gave a grim frown. "I don't believe you meant to. You were terrified at reliving that dreadful night. And in your fear and confusion, you lashed out at those you encountered."

A stricken look crossed Bridget's pale face. She looked away, staring into the fire as a slight tremor shook her bottom lip.

Part of Abigail felt pity for the dead woman, caught between the worlds of the living and the dead. What must it be like to face the dreadful torment of eternal solitude? Abigail wished she could reassure her she would find peace beyond the Veil. But nobody knew what lay in that shadowy realm. She was only certain that Bridget didn't belong here. Bridget had already killed once; she would do so again. With Judah gone, she was doomed to roam these silent halls for eternity. The loneliness would inevitably drive her mad and make her as murderous as her own killer had been.

"'Tis time you left here, Bridget," Abigail said. "Now that Judah's spirit is no more, you are free to—"

An invisible hand clamped tight on her throat.

Bridget shrieked as Judah Abbott's massive figure materialized before them.

Abigail's eyes bulged, and she gagged and gasped for air. The spirit's fingernails dug into her skin, his powerful fingers gouging her tendons. She scratched at the leather cord around her neck, fumbling for her protective talisman. But she couldn't get past Judah's huge hand and thick wrist.

Anna clutched the useless pistol and stared in horror as the malevolent spirit seized her mother and hauled her toward the foyer with murderous intent. She had been right; somehow, their spell hadn't worked. Something else was keeping Judah's spirit here, a bond too powerful for their magic to sever.

*Her…* whispered the shadowy voice in Anna's head. *'Tis her…*

Anna's muscles tightened. She understood at once.

She whirled and stared at Bridget in astonishment. "You! We had thought Judah brought you back to this inn year after year, but we were mistaken. *You* are keeping *him* here! As long as you remain in this place, his spirit will return for you!"

Bridget stared back at her, eyes wide with fright. "But I—"

Abigail's choked breaths rattled down to them as Judah dragged her up the stairs. Anna could hear her feet thrashing against the oak treads.

"You must end it, Bridget!" she cried. "Tonight! Right now! If you don't, more innocents will be swept up in your eternal tragedy and die! My *mother* will die!"

The reverberations of Judah's booming footsteps were less distinct now. He was approaching the third floor, hauling Abigail toward the bed in Room Nine.

Bridget's eyes were round with terror as she looked at Anna. "How? How can I stop it?"

"You must go willingly."

"Where?"

"Beyond the Veil."

Anna spun to the cabinet behind her. Shielding her eyes with one arm, she rammed the butt of the pistol into the pane and smashed the dingy glass. Shards tumbled to the floor at her feet. She snatched one up and drew it across the unblemished skin of her forearm. She flinched and sucked in a breath as a hot bolt of pain flashed up her arm.

From above came the crash of a door slamming shut. Judah had reached the bedroom at the end of the hall. There was the distant and muffled sounds of a desperate struggle as Abigail fought him off.

Blood seeped from Anna's wound as she closed her eyes and murmured the invocation she had heard her mother recite dozens of times. But she lost the precise intonation of the last words in a fog of panic. Her voice faltered, and she was crushed under a wave of despair.

She was powerless. Her mother was going to die.

The old voice scratched its way into her mind again. It whispered the forgotten words into her ear. Anna repeated them aloud, and they flooded her with an ecstatic surge that made her flesh quiver and her knees tremble beneath her.

A deathly chill filled the sitting room.

Anna opened her eyes.

Her mother's Familiar had returned.

The ghostly mist drew itself together, coalescing into the spectral figure of a young woman. She might have been pretty but for the dreadful hollow holes of her eyes.

Bridget stared at the vaporous figure.

"Go with her, Bridget," Anna urged. "Don't be afraid. She will guide you through the Veil from this place. Go with her and be at peace."

Upstairs, the furious struggle on the third floor had gone ominously quiet.

"Please, Bridget!" Anna cried. "You must go now before it's too late!"

The apparition opened her arms, beckoning.

Bridget wavered a moment longer. She took an uncertain step, her legs wobbling as she crossed the room into the spirit's embrace. The ghostly woman evaporated the instant they touched, dissolving into an ethereal white mist that coiled around Bridget like the vines of a rosebush. There was a blinding burst of otherworldly light that forced Anna to shield her eyes with her forearm.

A heartbeat later, they were gone.

The deserted inn went deathly silent.

Anna let the captive air from her lungs.

Up on the third floor, a door slammed open. There came a furious pounding of feet as Abigail came racing down the stairs.

"What happened?" She was breathless as she swept into the sitting room. Her face was flushed and there were livid handprints around her throat where Judah had been strangling the life from her. "Where did he go? Where is Bridget?"

"She crossed over." Anna was still reeling from the adrenaline slamming though her veins. "And Judah went after her."

Abigail stalked across the room and pierced her daughter with a gaze so intense it frightened her. "You knew the spell wouldn't work. How? How did you know?"

Anna stared at her, shocked by the naked gravity of her mother's tone.

"Tell me!" Abigail demanded.

Withering under her mother's stern glare, Anna suddenly sensed she shouldn't speak of the voice that had guided her, the dark guardian that whispered to her when she was most vulnerable.

"Judah loved her enough to follow her here through a terrible storm," she replied. "He ended both of their lives because he couldn't have her. Even in death, he would follow her anywhere."

Abigail's gaze held her transfixed a moment longer. Anna felt a shiver of fear run through her. *She knows! She knows the truth behind your lie…*

But then, Abigail's hard glare softened. "You were right, Anna. It appears you *are* ready to join me. There is a tavern nearby; I believe you have earned a woman's drink."

Abigail gave her daughter a smile, but it was all teeth and there was a tightness in her cheeks that made it feel false. Though they never spoke of it, Anna would long remember the unvoiced sentiment she had seen in her mother's eyes that night:

*Something about you frightens me, my child…*

*Author's Note*

Thank you, dear reader, for the generous gift of your time and attention. If you enjoyed these stories and would like to see more, please consider taking a moment to leave a quick review on Amazon and/or Goodreads. A kind word from a reader like you is one of the best ways you can support independent authors and is very much appreciated.

Until next time, look under the bed, close the closet door, and whatever you do, don't turn around…

# BOOKS BY MICHAEL PENNING

*Book of Shadows* **Series**
Novels:
*All Hallows Eve*
*The Suicide Lake*
*The Wolf Society*
*The Black Testament*

Companion Stories:
*The Damnation Chronicles*

**Other Novels**
*Solitude*

Michael Penning is a bestselling author and award-winning screenwriter of horror and dark fiction. He has been obsessed with all things dark and spooky since before he could finish his own sack of trick-or-treat candy. When he's not coming up with creative ways to scare the hell out of people, he enjoys traveling, photography, and brewing beer. He lives in Montreal with his wife and daughter. For updates and free giveaways, visit www.michaelpenning.com and follow Michael on social media @michaelpenningauthor.

Made in the USA
Middletown, DE
29 June 2024

56534762R00038